Beauty, Her Basket

Greenwillow Books

An Imprint of HarperCollinsPublishers

Amistad

Beauty, Her Basket

By **Sandra Belton**

Illustrated by **Cozbi A. Cabrera**

It sits on the table in the sea room. Next to the window where we can hear the water playing. Where the smell of the sea comes in and makes my stomach dream.

Every morning it's where the flowers rest first. That's what Nana says they are doing. Later she puts them all over the house.

Today the flowers match the colors of my dress. I take one for my hair. Nana gives me a hug and tells me I'm beautiful.

"A truth mouth, me," she says, and squeezes tight.

"And today you're going to tell me about the basket. That's true, too, right, Nana?" I say when I squeeze back.

"Soon as I hot the water for tea, we go. Now, rest you mouth, child."

I stick my nose inside the basket as far as it can go. I want to smell its secrets.

"What you smelling is the sea," says Uncle Richard. "Everything here is kin to the sea."

Uncle Richard's fingers pull and stretch while he talks. "That there's a sea grass basket. Folks around here make them from grasses that grow by the sea."

"Sea grass basket." I say the name quiet in my mouth and like how it sounds.

"Mama calls them sweetgrass baskets," says Victor. My cousin. He's visiting Nana for the summer like I am.

I like how that name sounds, too. But I don't say it soft for myself to hear. I only make a face at Victor.

Then I think about the name I like best of all.

"This here Beauty, Her Basket," Nana says.

And today she promises to tell me why.

When Nana tells Victor to walk with us, I ask why. I want just us to go walking. Just her and me.

"Victor, he family like you. We all family together," Nana says.

I try something different to keep him away.

"But, Nana," I say, "Victor wants to go shrimping with Uncle Richard. And you need shrimp for the gumbo, right?"

"We go shrimping early this morning while you and Victor sleeping. Shrimp out the shell and ready for the pot."

Nana makes her hand dance at Victor. Telling him to come on and to keep up. I walk fast beside Nana and hope he'll keep dragging behind.

For a long time we just walk without talking. I like listening to the sea and try to make the sound.

Shshroooommmmm. Shshroooommmmm.

Victor sees someone and runs ahead. "Hey, Henry," he calls.

He catches up with the boy we see on the beach almost every day. I think maybe the two of them will go off and play.

Nana calls to the boy. "Henry," she says, "your Nana Mary near?"

Henry points to a house hiding in the trees. Nana heads that way, and I follow her. I feel the sand Victor and Henry kick on my legs and know they're following, too.

I stay in the yard with Victor and Henry and hope Nana doesn't want to visit for a long time. Then she tells me to come up on the porch to see what Miss Mary is doing.

When I get close, I see Miss Mary making a basket. The flat, underneath part of it is like Beauty, Her Basket!

I can tell from Nana's eyes that she knows what I'm thinking.

"Yeah, child," she says. "Another Beauty, Her Basket."

Miss Mary shows me the pieces she's twisting and turning together.

"This here de palm leaf," she says, "this here longleaf pine needle, and this sea grass."

"Where you learn how to make this, Miss Mary?" I ask.

"From my Nana," Miss Mary says. "Like she learn from hers."

I want to ask how the first Nana of all learned, but then Henry says something I can't believe.

"I learned from my mama!"

I start laughing and look at Victor, who I think is laughing, too. But he's not.

"What you laughing at?" Victor says. "I learned from my mama. What's so funny about that?"

Now everybody's laughing but me. I try not to show how I feel, but Nana can tell.

"Don't be giving the long eye, child," Nana says. She rubs her hand down my back. "You learn like them."

We sit for a long time on Miss Mary's porch. I still want to know about Beauty, Her Basket and if all of the baskets are called that. But I have to keep my mind on what my hands are supposed to do.

I don't mind, though. Every time I lean close to pull the grass tight, I can smell the sea on my hands.

Nana says it's time to leave and that we'll come another time to do more.

I tell Miss Mary, "Thanks," and hope my hug says it, too.

This time when Victor and Henry run and kick sand, I do the same thing. They make the sound of the sea with me.

Shshroooommmmm. Shshroooommmmm.

Nana sits on one of the sand hills and watches.

The sky makes me think of the shrimp we're going to have for dinner. I ask Nana if we're going home soon.

"Yeah, soon," Nana says. "The sun almost de red for down."

I sit beside Nana. When Victor and Henry come, too, I don't mind. For a long time we sit, feeling the wind on our faces.

The wind makes the grass and trees wave like fans. Nana's hair, too. I ask Nana if my hair looks the same way.

"The wind fan everything," she says. She reaches into the sand and throws some into the air.

"Way back in the olden day, the wind help Beauty, Her Basket fan the rice," Nana says. She throws more sand into the air.

"What do you mean?" Victor and Henry and I ask at the same time.

Nana's voice is quiet. "The old blacks. The ones made to slave. Like the father before my father and the father before that. They bring the secrets of growing the rice with them from Africa and know Beauty, Her Basket will help."

Nana looks into the wind. "Think about that, my babies," she says. "See the picture."

I look up into the sky like Nana is doing. Victor and Henry do, too. At first I don't see anything but a trail of clouds. I wonder if Victor and Henry can see something else.

Nana keeps talking. "The old ones bring the knowing of how to grow the rice like they bring the knowing of how to make the basket."

I keep looking up while I listen. I look hard to see the picture like Nana says.

"They bring the knowing of how to make nets for catching the fish. Like Uncle Richard make the nets on this side."

I see a gull flying across a cloud and imagine Uncle Richard throwing his net across the water.

"The old blacks bring a lot of knowing with them. How to carve the wood and build the boat and make the pots for carrying the water from the sea."

Nana stops talking, but we still keep looking at the sky.

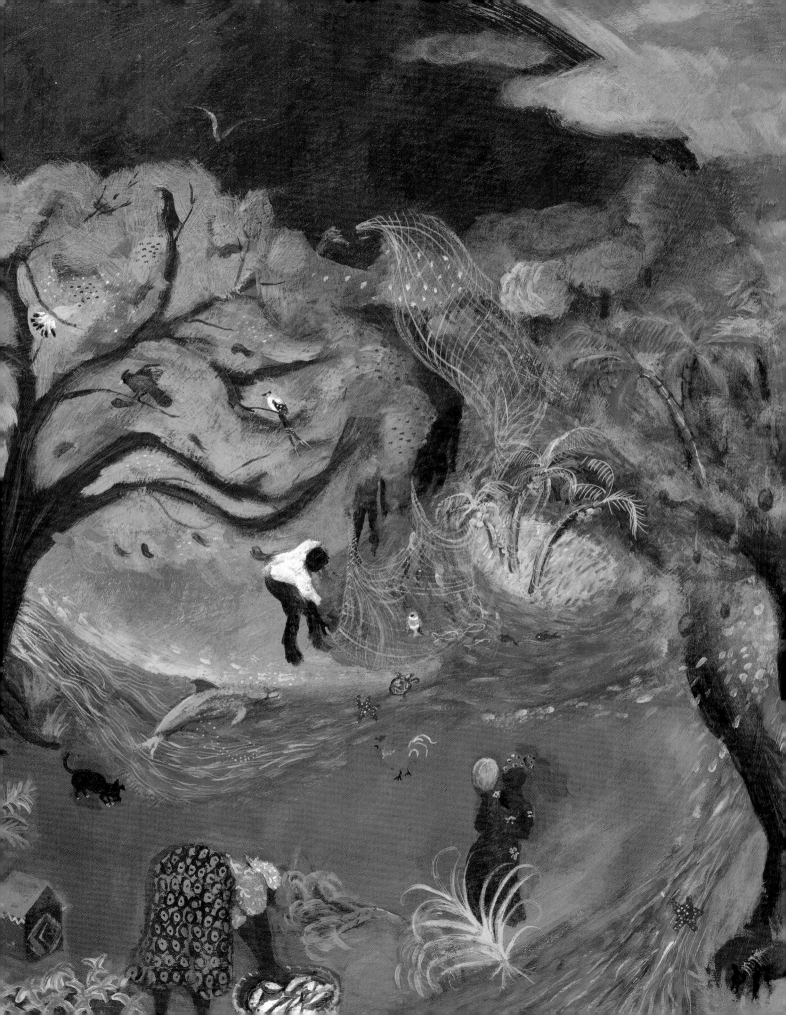

Nana touches the flower in my hair. "Every morning I put a flower in my basket. Beauty from this side. Something to go with beauty from the other side. Beauty, Her Basket."

I look into Nana's face. I want to understand.

Her voice is soft. "So much ugly in the slave times. Much too much ugly. But the basket like the flower— always a child of beauty. No matter what."

Then I understand. "Beauty, Her Basket," I say, soft like Nana.

Nana rubs her hand down my face. "Like you and Victor," she says. "Beauty, my babies."

Nana gets up and shakes the sand from her dress. "Look here. The sun almost de red for down! Time for me to tie my mouth and us to get home," she says.

I hear Nana's words and know she's holding on to something else from Africa. I smile and catch her hand.

"I'll help with the gumbo, Nana," I say.

Nana looks at me out the corner of her eyes. "What you know about cooking gumbo?" she says.

"Lots," I say. "I help Mama at home all the time. And I'm a truth mouth, me."

The wind mixes our laughing with the sound of the sea.

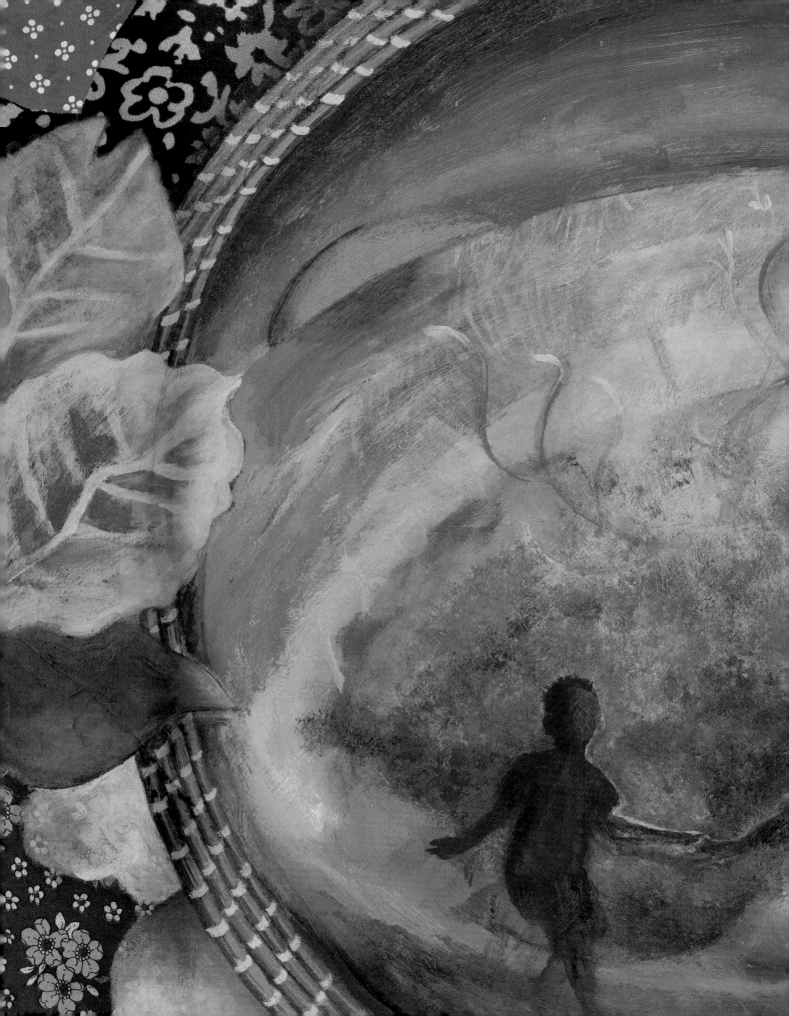

For
Bernadine Johnson Bolden
of nearby-sweetgrass country,
and always for Allen Douglass
—S. B.

Very special thanks to Kate Nyquist
for passing the name to my imagination
—S. B.

Beauty, Her Basket
Text copyright © 2004 by Sandra Belton
Illustrations copyright © 2004 by Cozbi A. Cabrera
Amistad is an imprint of HarperCollins Publishers, Inc.
All rights reserved. Manufactured in China
by South China Printing Company Ltd.
www.harperchildrens.com

Acrylics were used to prepare the full-color art.
The text type is 15-point Arrus.
The display type is Isadora Regular.

Library of Congress Cataloging-in-Publication Data

Belton, Sandra.
Beauty, her basket / by Sandra Belton ; pictures by Cozbi A. Cabrera.
p. cm.
"Greenwillow Books."
Summary: While visiting her grandmother in the Sea Islands, a young girl
hears about her African heritage and learns to weave a sea grass basket.
ISBN 0-688-17821-9 (trade). ISBN 0-688-17822-7 (lib. bdg.)
1. Gullahs—Juvenile fiction. [1. Gullahs—Fiction. 2. Sea Islands—Fiction.
3. Grandmothers—Fiction. 4. Sweetgrass baskets—Fiction. 5. Baskets—Fiction.
6. African Americans—Fiction.] I. Cabrera, Cozbi A., ill. II. Title.
PZ7.B4197 Be 2004 [E]—dc21 2003040599

10 9 8 7 6 5 4 3 2 1 First Edition

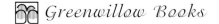 *Greenwillow Books*